THE ISLAND OF SKREE

UTT

JUNGLE
OF UTT

THE Jungle OF UTT

A series of adventure stories

This book belongs to

Welcome to Utt

on the Island of Skree

THE UTT JUNGLE AIRLINE

Written by Cameron Thomas

Illustrations by Andrej Krystoforski

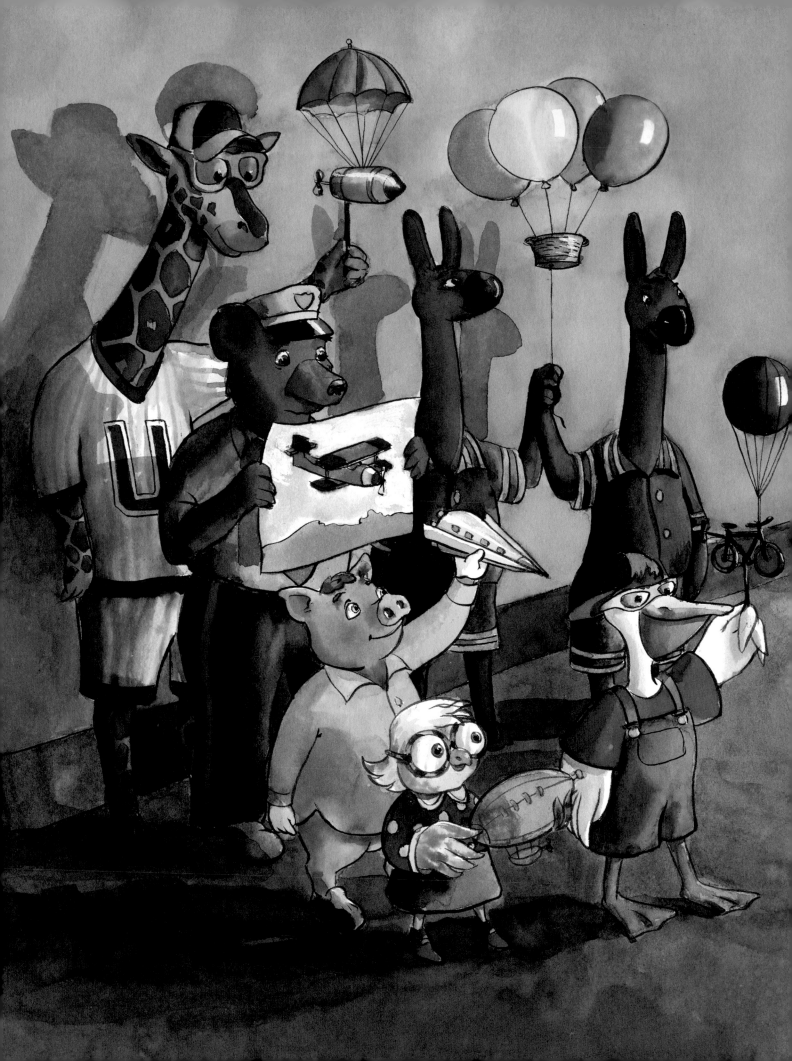

In the Jungle of Utt, on the Island of Skree
(Just a dot on the map in the Sassaway Sea),
The town folk had brought some ideas to the Mayor,
About building an airship, to fly through the air
So that the people who live in outlying terrain
Can visit the big city now and again.
So they talked it all over, and drew up a plan,
And the next morning work on the airship began.

"The first thing we need," said the Mayor to the crew,
"Is a framework, and that will take lots of bamboo.
We'll need a large basket of wickerwork too,
(That's a job that perhaps the young people could do)
And we'll cover it all with broad leaves sewn together,
But it must be well made; we might get stormy weather."

So they laid down a keel, just like building a ship,
And alongside they placed the bamboo, strip by strip,
Which they bent from each end, to make sort of a wheel,
Of each strip, which was then tightly tied to the keel.
'Til the main frame was finished, and there in the dale,
It looked like the bones of a gigantic whale.
And the sightseers, gazed up, in wonder and awe,
They'd never seen anything like it before.

Then some tall trees were cut, and were made into towers,
And the frame placed between them, it took many hours,
But it had to be hoisted above the ground so,
That the passenger basket could be tied below.
Then the seats were put in, and pilot's controls,
And the rudder fixed in its appropriate holes,
And a cover of palm leaves was sewn into place,
While the Mayor looked on, with a smile on his face.

The propeller was fixed to a shaft at the rear,
Which in turn was attached to a chain and a gear,
And the whole thing was driven by pedals inside
The compartment in which the ship's aircrew would ride.
And it looked like the only thing now left to do,
Was to make the selection of pilot and crew.

Pinky the Pig was the first to apply
For the pilot's position, he wanted to fly,
And the Mayor said "That's fine, if you like aviation,
I'll teach you a few things about navigation."
And then the two Llamas, both eager and keen,
Asked if they could be pedallers of this new machine.

They were both very fit, for they played lots of sport,
And they joined fitness classes the coach Giraffe taught,
Then the bike riding Pelican asked to be hired,
Saying he could take over, if someone got tired.
And the people agreed, and said it was just fine,
For this group to be crew of the Utt Jungle Line.

Having made the selection of pilot and crew,
A test flight of course was the next thing to do,
But first a big fire was built, so that hot air
Could be piped in to lift the ship up in the air,
And as more and more hot air came in through the hose,
The ship lifted off, and the air hole was closed.
And the people all cheered, and they waved a good-bye
As the ship slowly rose in the afternoon sky.

When the airship had flown to a reasonable height,
The pig tried the rudder to left and to right.
He was nervous at first, but he soon got the feel,
And in no time he felt quite at home at the wheel,
While behind him the Llamas were grinding out power;
That was driving them forward at twelve miles an hour.
They stayed up a long time, for they knew it was best
To give every control there, a very good test.

Next day, in the field, at the south end of town,
The ship was prepared, and a crowd had come down,
And a lot had bought tickets, they wanted to be
The first in Utt Jungle to fly around Skree.
And there in Utt Jungle, by morning's first light,
The airship took off on its historic flight.

The airship flew on under two Llama power,
As they turned the propeller round hour after hour.
And the pelican filled in, and pedaled with zest
When one of the two of them needed a rest.
And the passengers looked all about them in awe,
They'd never been up in an airship before.

They were really excited, for now they could see,
Spread out far below them, the Island of Skree.
And just up ahead, looking mighty and proud,
Mount Thimble was pushing its head through the clouds.

The crew was so busy at what they were doing,
That nobody noticed the bad weather brewing,
As the clouds round Mount Thimble enveloped the ship
The Pig got quite worried, they might hit the tip.
But the wind blew them past it, but so far off track,
That he just couldn't work out the way to get back.

So he said to his crew: "We'll fly east over Skree,
Until we arrive at the Sassaway Sea."
But although the two Llamas worked on with a will,
They couldn't make headway, and nearly stood still,
For the wind that had blown them so far off their course,
Was now blowing head on, with much stronger force.
And there they were, over the coastline of Skree,
When the wind changed, and blew them out over the sea.

Back in Utt, in the meantime, the people were trying
To stay calm, while they waited for friends who were flying.
The airship was due back at quarter past three
Having made the long trip round the Island of Skree.
But when three fifteen came not a thing was in view,
So by now they were thinking, the ship's overdue.

But the Mayor said, "Don't worry, they'll be quite alright.
Bad weather, perhaps, made them stop for the night.
I'll ask Hiram T. Quink to put on his red shoes
And search for the ship and then bring us the news."

Back on board it was late, they were losing the light,
As the big airship drifted on, into the night.
They drifted for hours, and were far out to sea,
And there wasn't a sign of the Island of Skree.
And the airship had dropped, and in morning's first glow
They could make out the waves just a few feet below.

Then the Pig, looking out, said, "We have got to get higher
But to get more hot air we must first make a fire."
But this was impossible, they could all see,
As they floated out over the Sassaway Sea.
And to make matters worse, it had started to hail,
As the wind got much stronger now, blowing a gale.

Then the Pig saw outside, a familiar form,
It was Hiram T. Quink, bravely fighting the storm.
He was pointing to something below, in the sea,
And the crew all looked down to see what it might be.
Then one of the pedalling Llamas looked out
And he saw a dark shape, and then let out a shout.

"We're up here," cried the Llamas, and gave a loud hale,
And one said to the Pig, "Look, that's Walter the Whale."
And the whale, sure enough, knew the two Llamas too,
And asked them the trouble, and what he could do.
So the Llamas said, "What if we drop you a rope,
Could you tow the ship back to the island? - we hope.
We've been blown off our course when it started to pour,
And we can't fight the wind and get back to the shore."

"Drop the rope right away," answered Walter the Whale,
"Make a loop on the end to fit over my tail,
You're not very far from the Island of Skree,
But in this heavy rain it's not easy to see."
So the crew dropped the rope down to Walter the Whale,
And Hiram T. Quink looped it over his tail.

And despite the storm's fury he finished his chore
And towed them back safe to the Sassaway Shore.
Then he bid them goodbye, and a safe journey home,
Before swimming back through the breakers and foam.

But the ship couldn't climb, they were low on hot air,
So they just skimmed the tree tops, to Utt Jungle square.
And when the big crowd saw the airship appear
They sighed with relief, and they gave a loud cheer,
As the pilot pushed down on the lever to land,
And the Utt Jungle airship obeyed his command.

The Llamas stopped pedalling, reducing the power,
As the crew dropped the ropes which were tied to the tower,
Then the hatch opened up, and the flight crew appeared,
And the passengers too, and again they all cheered.

The Utt Jungle band played a welcome home song,
And the Mayor thanked the eagle for being so strong,
And flying, in spite of the inclement weather
To bring Walter the Whale and the aircrew together,
And he added, "This airline is just what we need."
(And the Llamas in purple pajamas agreed).

THE Jungle OF UTT

- More books to come -

ISLAND GRAND PRIX
WALTER THE WHALE
THE RAILWAY TO THE SEA
THE CONQUEST OF THIMBLE MOUNTAIN
KIDNAPPED
WATER, WATER EVERYWHERE
UTT GETS A FIRE BRIGADE
WEEKEND AT THE BEACH
HIRAM IN TROUBLE
FLYING SAUCER
FIRE
THE LOST KANGAROOS
WALTER GOES HOME
100 YEARS OF UTT
WEEKEND WITH A WHALE
PLAN FOR A CITY
THE UTT GENERAL ELECTION
BARNABY BUILDS A BOAT
THE LONG VOYAGE HOME

Published by:
MGT Publishing Inc.
125 Main Street West
Grimsby ON. Canada
L3M 1S1

Copyright:
The United States Copyright Office, The Library of Congress.

Copyright Office
Ottawa, Ontario, Canada

First published in 2004

ISBN 0 921800 03 7

Digitally Composed
by David Pereira

Printed in China

Check out our web site at:
WWW.jungleofutt.com